A Different Reality

tales of mystery

by

marc lensly

Copyright © Marc Lensly 2005

PUBLISHER'S NOTE

All rights reserved. No part of this book may be reproduced, stored in a retrieval system or transmitted in any form or means without the prior consent of the publisher, except for a review where brief passages may be quoted to be printed in the media by a reviewer.
This is a work of fiction. Names, characters, places and incidents are the product of the author's imagination or are used fictitiously.

www.marclensly.com

for pascal

the best friend one can ask for

*

for my family

**

thank you all for your kind support
and for reminding me every now and then
not to give up my dream

***

CONTENTS

1. Connected　　　　　　　　　p. 7

2. Ghost Hunt　　　　　　　　p. 23

3. The Encounter　　　　　　　p. 31

4. Volunteer on Saturday　　p. 39

5. Gemini　　　　　　　　　　　p. 61

6. Rachel　　　　　　　　　　　p. 87

7. Anna's Child　　　　　　　p. 105

Connected

'No, Mother!' said Stephen firmly, more annoyed than actually cross. 'Can't talk now, have to go. Love you!' and he pressed the red telephone icon on his cell phone to end the conversation.

'For crying in a bucket,' he mumbled to himself out loud, 'I'm thirty-two years old, Mom. Stop bugging me like this, will you?'

A knock at his office door made him look up.

'Come in.' A young clerk entered and fiddled with a file in his hands.

'Excuse me, Mr. Waters, but Mr. Henry would like to see the application form of "Harold & Harold". He'd like to know if you've approved the account or not.'

'Justin,' said Stephen with a friendly smile, 'do you know that I've been working here three months now and you're the only one who still calls me "Mister Waters"?'

'Oh … sorry Mister … uh … Stephen.'

'Now, that wasn't so hard, now was it?' smiled Stephen again. 'Here you go,' and he handed Justin a file which he took out of his out tray. 'All signed and approved.'

'Thanks, Miste … uh .. Stephen,' said Justin as he took the file and left the office.

Stephen sat down behind his desk and sighed. It was a sigh of happiness. For the first time in months, he actually felt happy and had a new, fresh jest for life.

A very unfortunate tragedy about six months earlier made him have a good look at his life. There he was, eight years in the same job after his university education. Oh, he was happy with his job and he actually had a flourishing career, but the tragedy made him decide to just up and go. To start a new, unknown future.

Immediately he started looking for employment in the big city, hundreds of kilometres away from where he had been for the previous eight years. He could not believe his luck when he got the first job that he applied for via an ad in a national newspaper. Maybe Lady Luck was starting to smile on him, he thought.

Things did not quite work out with Estelle, much to his annoyance. How he sometimes disliked it when his mother was correct in her predictions.

'Stephen, my boy,' she said one evening while they were having a drink after dinner, 'that girl is no good for you, I tell you.'

'Mom, please …' But his mother carried on.

'I'm telling you! She's a no good, money-seeking, blood-sucking leech of a hussy!'

'Mom!' he shouted, 'I just happen to love Estelle, okay? And I expect you to respect that, you hear me?!'

'You'll expect nothing of the sort,' she continued, 'mark my words tonight. A no good hussy, she is.'

Stephen left that evening feeling very angry. He knew that his mother meant well, but he thought she could have had a bit more tact. And then what happened?

A few weeks down the line, he came to realise that his mother was right. Estelle was a no good, money-seeking, blood-sucking leech of a hussy.

He smiled as he thought back to that evening he told his mother that he had broken up with Estelle. He was expecting a long lecture from her. But she just took off her glasses, looked at him, smiled softly and said 'Good, now you can carry on with your life.'

That was exactly what Stephen did. He carried on with his life and now, after so many months, he was happy again. He had a great job; he liked the people he worked with; they liked him; he bought a little house just outside the city and he even started playing tennis again. Life was just grand.

Then, of course, there was Caroline.

He met her a few weeks after he had started his new job. She also worked in a bank, a few blocks away from the bank where he was working.

About a week after his first day on the job, he discovered a quaint little coffee house which he started frequenting every lunch time. One day he noticed a lovely young woman in her late twenties.

Quite a catch, he thought to himself, but definitely spoken for. He could not have been more wrong.

After a few days he saw that she sat alone, most of the time. Sometimes a female friend accompanied her, but in general she sat all by herself. Not being a shy type of person, Stephen quickly made her acquaintance and after a mere three weeks they went on their first date.

Now it was about two months later and they got along splendidly. As a matter of fact, Stephen felt in his gut that this woman was the woman that he'd like to spend the rest of his life with.

Saturday afternoon.
Stephen and Caroline had an appointment at two o'clock at the tennis club where he was a member. They had been playing there together, shortly after their first official date. Daniel and Marty were their tennis partners, or rather opponents, for the afternoon. That was going to be a very decisive match. They had never managed to beat Daniel and Marty. Stephen decided that, should they win, it would be a sign from heaven that he should ask the big question. In other words, if they won, he was going to ask Caroline to marry him.

The four friends were sitting in the clubhouse, waiting for the court to become available; refreshing cool drinks all round and just chatting about nothing in particular. After a short while, Stephen excused himself and said that he had to go visit the gents' room. As he got up, his cell phone rang in his sport's bag.

At first he did not realise it was his cell phone, as he usually put it off when he goes to play tennis, even though he always took it with him.

'Stephen,' said Caroline, 'your phone.'

'Oh,' he replied with a puzzled look, 'sorry, didn't know it was mine. Such a nuisance sometimes. Let it ring.'

'But,' continued Caroline, 'it could be important. Go on, just answer it, you never know. Besides, our court has only just finished the first set. There's plenty of time.'

Stephen searched blindly in his sport bag until he eventually got hold of the phone. He started walking away from his party and looked at the little window on his cell phone.

The word 'MOM' was displayed.

He rolled his eyes, sighed a bit, hesitated a split second and then reluctantly pressed the green telephone icon on his phone.

'Yes, Mom, what is it?'

He listened for a while as the voice from the other side spoke to him. Because of the noise in the clubhouse, he decided to rather go outside.

'Hang on, too much noise here. I'm going outside quickly.'

Caroline could see Stephen speaking excitedly on the phone through the big clubhouse windows. She frowned as she saw him speaking anxiously and at one stage he dropped his hand to his side, whilst holding the phone tightly in a clenched fist. He once again brought the phone to his ear, said a few words and hung up.

When he returned after a few minutes, that is after a quick visit to the restrooms as well, he came back to join the others at the table.

'Who was on the phone?' asked Caroline.

'Nobody,' he said bluntly, 'it was nobody, really. Come on guys, let's go outside a bit. It's such a glorious day and the bunch on the court should be almost finished. Look! The other side is flattening them. Don't think they'll be too long now.'

It was a very intense match for the four players.

Daniel and Marty won the first set quite easily, as usual. The score was 6-2.

Stephen started thinking that maybe today was not the day, when all of a sudden his serve picked up. He felt a real Andy Roddick as he served ace after ace after ace. His serve was so impressive that even Daniel had to pay him a compliment.

'My!' exclaimed Daniel, 'if you carry on like that, you can go and enrol for Wimbledon next year, mate!'

Stephen just smiled. If only they knew how much was at stake here.

Stephen and Caroline won the second set 7-6 in a tie-break and then the real battle started.

After about another forty minutes of play and with four other very discontented people waiting for the tennis court to become available, Stephen and Caroline took the last set 8-6. They opted not to play a tie-break, just as if it were a professional match.

As Daniel and Marty started walking off the court, Caroline came running up to Stephen and kissed him passionately.

'Oh, Stephen, we're the new champions!' she laughed. Stephen smiled back and took her in his arms.

'I'd feel like a real champion if you'll accept something from me,' he said in a very serious voice.

'Oh? That sounds quite serious.'

Stephen took a thin ribbon tied around his neck. He tore the ribbon gently and he let something slip into the palm of his other hand. He held a most gorgeous diamond ring out to Caroline.

'I know maybe it's a bit early, as we've only been seeing one another a short while, but … would you marry me, Caroline?' he said with an expectant look in his eyes.

Tears welled up in Caroline's eyes.

'Oh, my darling, it's not a matter of forty-love, but a matter of game, set, match and love forever. Of course I'll marry you!'

They kissed passionately right there on the court and Daniel and Marty could not understand that they were that happy because they beat them.

Later that evening, after some rest and a good shower, the four friends met at the Jolly

Lobster for an evening out. It was only when they had their aperitifs that Stephen told them the good news.

Cheers of congratulations and felicitations went up and everybody in the restaurant turned their heads to see what all the happy commotion was about. Caroline shared her lovely diamond ring with Marty and the latter was mightily impressed. They all had a wonderful evening. An evening that they would not easily forget.

It was time for desert when the phone call came. The ring of a cell phone was quite audible, even though the restaurant was buzzing with activity.

Nobody at the table made an effort to answer. Daniel knew that they left their phone in the car and Caroline left hers at home. As the ringing continued, they all looked at Stephen.

'Well?' Marty said to Stephen, 'going to get that?'

'Not mine,' he laughed, but the ringing did not subside.

'Uh, Stephen, that's definitely yours,' said Caroline.

'Can't be, darling, I'm sure I left it in the car,' he replied, but started searching his jacket pockets. To his total disbelieve, his fingers touched his cell phone in the left inner pocket.

'I just don't believe this,' he mumbled. He took the phone out of his pocket and once again saw the word 'MOM' on the little screen.

'Excuse me, please,' he said, quite embarrassed and left the table to go outside, 'I have to take this quickly.'

Stephen went outside and halfway to the door pressed the green telephone icon again. He only spoke once he got outside.

'What is it now, Mother?' he asked quite angrily and carried on talking before there was an answer from the other side. 'I'm in the middle of dinner here!'

He listened attentively and replied very firmly.

'No, Mother! No! You can't meet her. You know that's impossible. I won't have it.' The voice from the other side said something again, but Stephen just put his foot down.

'No, Mother! I will not put her on the phone for you. No! Now please stop bothering me like this!' There was once again some talk on the other said, when Stephen's expression changed slightly into a more friendly composure.

'Yes, I know. Sorry, Mom. I know you mean well. But, believe me, I'm doing the right thing here.'

He still listened for a while, by then totally relaxed and with a smile on his face.

'Okay, Mom, thanks for phoning. Got to go now. Love you, okay?'

Once back in the restaurant, three inquisitive faces looked at him as he got to the table.

'Sorry, people, just a bit of business.'

And that's all he said about the phone call.

One year later.

After a fairytale wedding, exactly twelve months to the day after their engagement, Stephen and Caroline were walking around in London. They were on their honeymoon and enjoyed every single moment of it. Not only did they drink in their Anglo-Saxon heritage, delivered down from generation to generation, but they were also just enjoying each other's company. Away from home, away from work, away from friends. Just the two of them in this metropolis of a city. Culture, history, architecture, wining and dining. In other words, experiencing a most memorable honeymoon.

The two of them were sitting at a small table in a tiny restaurant located on the banks of the Thames, drinking tea. Both were lost in thought, when Caroline broke the silence.

'You know? I've been having such a fabulous time these passed few months, but I sometimes feel a bit selfish, enjoying life like this.'

'What ever do you mean, darling?' asked Stephen.

'Well, it's just that you've been treating me like a real, live princess and at times I forgot what a sad time it must have been for you.'

A question mark appeared on his forehead.

'Caroline, I'm as happy as can be. What gives you the idea that I might have been unhappy or sad?'

'Well, Stephen, I can't help but think of your Mom. You seemed quite upset when you told me about her passing away. And that in a sudden car crash. I just find it terrible that she never lived to see you getting married. How long ago did she die again?'

Stephen reflected for a moment before he answered.

'Darling, she died about three months or so before I met you. But … do you know what?' He smiled softly.

'What?' she asked in a tender voice.

'I know this might sound like a real cliché, but I always have the feeling that my mother was there with us on our wedding day. In spirit, that is,' he added quickly.

'Well, I know people believe that. I actually do too, you know.'

He smiled and gave her a kiss on the cheek.

'I know that my Mom is always looking out for me. I loved her dearly and I always will.'

They finished their tea and got up, after Stephen paid, and walked hand-in-hand along the promenade.

Suddenly his cell phone rang in his little moon bag.

'Oh, no!' he cried out, 'not on our honeymoon!'

'Just answer it,' laughed Caroline.

Stephen looked at the little window on his cell phone, as he always did and frowned. Two words were displayed.

It said 'ID withheld.'

He answered the phone, listened for a minute and then hung up.

'And?' enquired Caroline, 'who was it?'

'It was only my mah … uhm … it was just somebody who gave us her blessing, that's all,' said Stephen with a look of extreme happiness.

He looked at Caroline, took her in his arms and kissed her tenderly.

Ghost Hunt

Rick Renders put the phone down whilst a chill ran down his spine. This would be the first time that he would be able to plan a visit to go see an apparition. Up to now he had only investigated events documented by others and his occasional live experiences had always been coincidental; he just happened to be there, which he had always been glad about.

But this time, this time …

'It happened about two weeks ago, on Valentine's Day,' said Arthur Eidelman.

Rick could see that the man was still upset as he noticed how the man's hands were trembling while he lit a cigarette that he took from a crumbled-up packet of Camels; the latter coming out of a pocket of his leather, motorbike jacket.

'Just relax and tell me what happened,' said Rick, switching on the tape recorder.

'Okay,' replied Arthur and took a deep drag from his cigarette. 'As I've said, it was Valentines Day. Actually it was late evening. My girlfriend and I had a nice, romantic dinner at her apartment. But, as we both had to go to work the following day, we decided not to let the evening drag out too long. I left just before eleven o'clock on my motorbike. The little town where she stays is about twenty kilometres away from the next village. About five kilometres before one enters the village, there is a railway crossing. Now I know that it's very dark over there and therefore I'm always very careful when I approach the crossing.'

    He took another puff on his cigarette before he carried on.

    'Well, this night, when I slowed down at the railway tracks, the engine of my motorbike just cut out. I suddenly heard the screaming signal of a train approaching. I thought that the boom and the warning lights weren't working, because I didn't see the flashing warning lights, nor the boom coming down. Then it struck me like a cricket ball in the face. There was no train! I waited for a while, but then decided to get out of there, as I thought all of that was a bit creepy. I kick-started my bike without a problem. About a kilometre from there, I noticed a figure standing next to the road. I slowed down and saw that it was a young woman, dressed in a rather old-fashioned white dress. Well, I thought it was white anyway. Automatically I stopped and asked her what she was doing there so late at night, all by herself. I could see she was crying and she had terrible contortions on her face, as if she were in terrible pain. She replied that she had to get to the police station for some help. I didn't ask any more questions, but just told her to get on the back of the motorbike.'

By this time Arthur's cigarette was a mere stub, so he killed it in the ashtray and immediately lit up another one. He seemed a bit more relaxed as he continued.

'Once again I took off and just when I was about to enter the village, an indescribable, freezing cold feeling swept over me. I once again slowed down, just to make sure that the girl was all right, but … there was no girl! I looked around, backtracked the road all the way to where I had picked her up. Nothing.'

'What did you do then?' asks Rick.

'I went to the police station right away. There was this old policeman on duty. I told him the whole story, but he merely smiled and said "It was Sandra".'

'Yes,' the old policeman said, 'Sandra was her name. A young girl, just turned twenty-one. The night of her engagement party. 14 February 1965.'

'Do you know what happened?' asked Rick, tape recorder on. He didn't want to miss a thing.

'Yeah. Sad story it was. Sandra and her friend, I can't remember his name any more, got privately engaged at a restaurant in the town about twenty kilometres away from here. In those days the youngsters didn't always stay out that late and, after a nice evening, I suppose, they set off back home. Well, the intention was to go have a cup of coffee at Sandra's house and show the ring to her parents. Now, did you see the railway crossing about five kilometres out of town?'

'Yes,' Rick confirmed, still hanging onto every word the old policeman said.

'Right,' the old man continued, 'now in those days, there were regular power failures and other stupid things going wrong. Not like today where everything's computerised. It just so happened that on that specific night, for some or other reason, the electricity to the warning light did not work. And there was no boom in those days either. One had to be alert whenever one neared a crossing like that. To make a long story short, Sandra's fiancé's car hit a pothole, the tyre burst and they ended up on the railway tracks. They didn't see or hear the approaching train. Both of them still recovering from the shock of the blow out of the tyre, you see. The train smashed up the car and threw it off the tracks a few metres down the line. The machinist only managed to stop some distance further. In the meantime, Sandra was still alive, although in great pain. She crawled out of the car to go look for help.'

The old policeman leaned forward as if he was about to share some vital information with Rick.

'Now take note. Story has it that a passing car had picked her up, exactly where the young man picked up her ghost. Unfortunately, she died in the Good Samaritan's car, exactly where the young man said he had this cold feeling. Over the years a lot of people came to this very police station and told me similar stories. Stories of a girl at the side of the road. Once picked up, she stays in the car or whatever vehicle and then disappears on the spot where she actually died in 1965.'

It was the 14th of February, one year later.

Rick Renders was sitting in his car, waiting at the railway crossing. It was almost eleven o'clock at night. According to his calculations, Arthur Eidelman should have passed there more or less around that time.

Rick advanced slowly in his car and then, all of a sudden and in total disbelief, he saw her.

A pale, sad-looking girl in her early twenties.

He stopped and let the automatic window on the passenger's side down. He did not say anything. He switched on his tape recorder as well as the video camera, mounted on the dashboard.

'Could you please take me to the police station?' the girl pleaded with a sob in her voice.

Poor soul, Rick thought. He didn't pull over onto the side of the road; he merely stopped the car in the road and kept the engine running. He opened the door and she got into the passenger seat. Rick slowly pulled off.

'Sandra,' he said, 'please listen to me.'

'How do you know my name?'

'That's not important. I am here because I want to help you.'

'No!' she cried, 'I have to help, you can't do anything. I have to get help. Right now! Drive please, just drive! Fast!'

'Sandra, there's nothing you can do. He's already dead.'

'No!'

Her screams filled the night like the haunting sound of a wailing banshee.

'Yes, Sandra,' Rick continued, 'there's nothing you can do. Let it go. Let him go. Make it easy on yourself and find peace.'

The pale-looking girl was in agony with pain. Not only physical pain, but also pain in her heart.

'If only I could get to the police on time, they'd be able to send for an ambulance. He can be saved,' she sobbed.

'No, Sandra. That's not true. He died the minute the train hit the car. Stop searching for help. It has no use.'

He spoke to her with a soft, comforting voice.

She listened.

'Step out here, Sandra. Get out of the car right here and go find peace. Please.'

Sandra looks at him, but doubted for a short while. She then smiled faintly and opened the car door.

She realised that she had been a restless spirit for all those years. All she needed was to hear the truth and get a little guidance.

As she got out of the car, Rick realised that Sandra was busy disappearing; little by little she became invisible. A bright light suddenly replaced her figure and Rick just knew instinctively that Sandra's spirit had found rest and peace at last.

Rick Renders switched off his tape recorder and the video camera; he put his car into first gear and drove off.

Finally, he had the evidence of the existence of the supernatural.

And what a sad business it was.

The Encounter

The brilliance of the full moon painted the sky in a magnificent velvet blue that twinkled with uncountable microscopic jewels in the distance.

It was a fairly warm summer evening. Not too late and the weather perfect to take her snugly animal for a walk. She absolutely adored her tiny little dog and started whistling softly to get his attention.

A quick, short bark indicated that he was in the kitchen and not entirely satisfied with his current situation. Somehow expecting the cat to be in the vicinity too, she opened the door leading into the kitchen and saw that her suspicions were correct.

The big, grey cat was sitting on the working surface next to the stove. He had a look of pure annoyance on his face as he looked at the yapping fur-ball on the floor.

The cat came to the house quite a few months ago and just made himself comfortable as if invited. The whole family, except the dog of course, had adopted him straight away and he never regretted that he had chosen that house-hold as his new home.

The Encounter

The girl remembered that day very well too.

With a smile on her face she greeted her parents with a promise not to be too late. Everybody knew that the small city where they lived was a very safe place and it was quite alright to go far a walk in the moonlight, even in the late hours of the night.

At the end of their road a small opening between two houses allowed one to squeeze through a fence, with effect that one ended up in the meadows that surrounded the whole area. The meadows led all the way up to the forest that started at the foot of the mountain.

Although there was just about a zero-rating when it came to crime in the neighbourhood, she was still a bit reluctant to go into the forest at night. Not a person who scared easily, she would go for long walks there during the clarity of the day, but the evening was something totally different.

The clean, fresh air filled her lungs as she took a deep breath. She let a big sigh escape, which made her dog look at her with a question mark between his eyes.

Life was wonderful and carefree.

The Encounter

The young girl enjoyed living and being on this world. The beautiful moonlit evening astounded her so much that she, all of a sudden, realised that she had wondered all the way up the hill right up to the beginning of the forest. The little dog was running into the darkness of the trees; he did not need to be on a leash. With horror she thought that she had to go looking for him in the blackness of the woods.

With a strange sensation in her stomach she approached the flickering orange lights. At first, from a distance, she thought it was a small campfire, made under the trees by some young adventurers like herself. Feeling a bit scared, however, she did not dare go deeper into the woods.

It was when the irritating, buzzing noise commenced that her curiosity got the better of her.

Her dog came running towards her from between the small bushes under the trees. She uttered a faint yelp; it was almost an exact imitation of the noise her dog was making.

Now totally intrigued, she walked carefully closer to the orange, flickering lights until the strange vehicle, that was causing all the noise, was in full sight.

Never before had she seen anything like it.

A bit bigger than a car and twice the height of one. No windows and one single door of some sort indicated to her that, however the vehicle was operated, it surely was not in any normal way that she knew about.

Suddenly, someone behind her cleared his throat.

This time there was not time to utter a scream. She was frozen to the spot. For exactly how long she could not move, did not know; she only started turning around when she heard the soft coughing sound again. Whoever was behind her only tried to get her attention and nothing more; somehow she just knew that.

With slow, calculating movements, her eyes got fixated on the creature standing solemnly under a tree.

The flickering orange lights put him in clear view. It was the most hideous looking creature she had ever seen. Judging from the growth of hair on his face, she assumed that it belonged to the male species.

His strangely short arms, long legs and too many fingers on each hand made her look away for a second or two with slight disgust.

The creature also stared with admiration and awe at the ugliest specimen of a woman that he had ever seen. Her too long arms, awkwardly short legs were most prominent. Even more ridiculous looking was the tiny piece of fluff that she had picked up in the meantime. The little thing had ceased making some strange, snorting noises and was shaking violently.

'Excuse me, ... uh ...' he said, not sure how to address her, 'but I mean you no harm. Please believe me. I am only here to ask you to deliver a message on behalf of my people.'

With utmost surprise she realised that he was speaking English. A somewhat ancient dialect. Although a bit complicated, she managed to understand what he was trying to get across.

'I know,' she replied, 'I can feel that you are not an enemy. What is it that you want me to do?'

He was equally fascinated that he could understand her very simplified use of the English language.

They started talking and he explained how they had been observing planets in the universe for a suitable place for his people to go and live.

His world was on the verge of extinction through global warming; it had caused some areas of the planet to live in a constant, unbearable heat. Other areas started getting flooded because of melting glaciers; the eternal snow on the mountains had also melted causing landslides, mudslides and floods all over, killing hundreds of thousands of inhabitants.

His whole planet was heading for disaster.

She, in turn, informed him how her planet had similar problems decades before, but through intensive research and ultra-modern technology, they eventually found a solution to the disaster that was threatening her planet.

His explanation of how he managed to override the radar systems and to land in the forest after leaving the main spaceship, hidden behind the mountain, the girl started realising that all those stories about UFO's that everybody had heard of through the years, were all true.

All the insinuations that the governments from all over conspired to suppress the existence of alien life forms, were also fact and not fiction. This newfound revelations filled her with excitement as well as with rage.

They talked for quite some time and eventually he went into the little craft and came back with a black, sealed plastic file.

'This is an explanation to your governments, as well as an apology for invading the privacy of your planet. But, in short, we need a world to relocate ourselves peacefully where we can start a new, safe life. I will return to this same spot in thirty days. I know it's not a long time for your leaders to make a decision, but time is really pushing. And,' he said with a pleading look in his eyes, 'please come alone if you could. I know I'm not in a position to make demands, but it would honestly be appreciated.'

After assuring him of complete secrecy, she gave him a kiss on his forehead, trying to avoid his ugly face.

They said goodbye with a shake of hands.

The Encounter

The man started entering the strangely looking craft when the girl called him back.

'I totally forgot to ask,' she said, 'what is your planet called?'

The man answered very simply.

'Earth. My planet is called EARTH.'

Volunteer on Saturdays

An early Saturday morning sun peered through the curtains in Mandy's chaotic bedroom. A few of her friends came over last night and, as all adolescent teenagers should behave, it was an unforgettable evening of laughter, boy stories, pizza eating, fashion discussions and then, of course, more boy stories.

She still felt like sleeping a little, but knowing that it was Saturday made her sit up in her bed very quickly. An eerie, but somehow exciting feeling filled her insides.

Then she remembered.

Today was going to be the first encounter with the sick old lady living in that dilapidated old house in the clearing, a couple of hundred meters from the old graveyard when you enter the town from the main road.

She has been doing volunteer work for the past two years and she realised that it gave her such a tremendous feeling of self-satisfaction and tranquillity knowing that she was doing something useful with her life, even at such a young age. Being the only child in the household made her mother, widow since the horrible death of her father, quite protective.

Nevertheless, her dear mother consented when she approached her with the idea that she would like to do volunteer work in her spare time at the local community centre.

In the beginning she merely helped out at the old-age home in Smith Street. Washing the dishes, folding blankets, preparing tea and other miscellaneous duties just to ease the workload of the permanent staff.

After a couple of months, the matron of 'Everyday Sunshine' had asked her if she would mind visiting some of the old people Saturday mornings. Of course she was overjoyed and immediately committed herself.

Without any reluctance, she climbed out of bed and opened the curtains to let the glory of the morning fill her bedroom.

'Mandy,' her mother called from the kitchen, 'breakfast is ready!'

It only took Mandy a couple of minutes to get dressed in something casual. After washing her face and a brisk brush of her hair, she dashed off to the awaiting morning meal.

'Your bedroom in order, dear?' her mother asked, knowing that it was not.

'Oh Mom, can't I come and clean it this afternoon?' she asked with a most pleading look on her face.

'Do I have to answer that, young lady?' her mother replied with a trace of a smile round the edges of her mouth.

Mandy knew very well that she wouldn't be allowed out of the house before the said bedroom was in order. She also knew that she would clean it before she left anyway.

It was worth a try, though. Mother and daughter had a good understanding and that was something they both treasured. It didn't take long before the teenager's room was in a liveable condition again. After a nice hug and a promise not to be too late, Mandy left for the little, though ominous looking house on the clearing near the village cemetery.

A welcoming sun beat down on her face as she walked toward the direction of the little cemetery. As usual Mandy felt quite happy from within, but today there was a different feeling that she just couldn't place. A quick glance at her watch made her walk a little faster.

Punctuality is one of her strong points and she would not want her new 'friend' to be disappointed should she show up late. The term 'friend' was something she used to prefer to call all the old people she visited.

Normally she would encounter a friend or two on the way on her weekly visitations, but awkwardly enough, she realised she never saw anyone until she reached the tattered, wooden front gate of the old house.

It was a big, grey cat that she saw sitting in front of the wooden door that would lead her into yet another old person's, or 'friend's' home.

Bessie Mangers proved to be a nice old lady with an obvious life experience too complex for the young Mandy to understand. Thanks to her peculiar sense of love for her neighbour, she did not seem to feel a bit uneasy in the old lady's company.

Bessie spoke with an accent totally unknown to her, and with a slight speech deficiency. Having worked with a lot of senior citizens before and sick old people, she did not pay too much attention to it at first. It wasn't until her second visit that Mandy started feeling a bit uneasy in the company of Bessie.

In the meantime she carried on with various chores and her new 'friend' seemed to be pleased. This was more than enough for Mandy and she left with an exhilarant feeling of self-satisfaction when she went home later that afternoon.

Mandy's best friend, Gwyneth, popped in the following Friday afternoon to find out how everything was at the little old lady's house the previous Saturday.

They had a long, pleasant chat. Mandy, however, did not say anything about the strange feeling she had at certain moments while she was in the little ghost house, as all the children from school called it.

Maybe it was better to keep it to herself, she thought. A positive outlook on life, like she had, was definitely not going to be spoiled by an immature emotion such as this. She decided to keep it to herself.

The second visit to Bessie's was very much the same as the first. After preparing her a little brunch with some lemonade, Mandy told Bessie that she was going to study for a while in the lounge as she had a History test on the Monday. Bessie already told her beforehand that she was going to have a lie-down after a small bite.

After approximately forty-five minutes Mandy started dozing off in the big, comfortable armchair in the corner of the measly furnished lounge.

The strange sound emanating from the tiny and only bedroom in the house sounded like a person trying to speak under water. It was more a gurgling sound than actual speech, but the irregularity of it must have penetrated the sub-conscious mind of the young girl sleeping in the chair in the tiny living room.

At first she thought she was dreaming, but the cold feeling that she had in her heart made her realize that she was busy waking up and that she was indeed hearing those strange noises. A sudden fear entered her system as she all of a sudden thought that maybe Bessie was having same kind of a stroke and that she was drowning in her own saliva.

Volunteer on Saturdays

This was a situation that she has never been in before. She rose very quietly from the chair and advanced to the bedroom with unsteady legs. The sight that greeted her made her stop in her tracks. There was a dressing table in the corner of the old lady's bedroom that one could see from the passage leading from the lounge to the bedroom.

The big mirror upon the dresser reflected an old, naked lady, bending backwards like an eighteen year old gymnast; she was having convulsions, or so Mandy thought, while she was uttering the most horrible noises as if she were choking on something. Mandy wanted to rush to her aid, but just could not move.

It was what happened then, that frightened Mandy more than anything has ever frightened her before. She knew she had to move; get away before Bessie saw her. However, she stood perplexed and could not look away from the mirror.

Then the old lady's eyes caught hers in the mirror.

Mandy just could not scream …

The whole town was devastated when they found out about the disappearance of Mandy.

Her mother was without solace. She just couldn't believe that anyone would want to hurt her little girl.

But nothing was going to take the little flicker of hope away from her. She believed that as long as there was no evidence, nothing actually did happen to Mandy. She might still come to the door and apologise for being late.

Others felt differently, especially one particular old lady who told everyone she had met until then, how her son had abandoned her, by renting the little house for her and then set off for Europe, leaving her destitute.

Gwyneth listened attentively while the fragile looking Bessie told her about her sad life with her only son. A life of forever moving around. In and out of old age and nursing homes, like some people would change their underpants. Left all by herself for weeks on end in an old, scruffy apartment.

After years of wandering about, he rented the old house near the cemetery for her and left her to her own devices. As she was telling Gwyneth all this, she started having tears in her eyes.

'Yes dear,' she said, 'just as I thought I could settle down at last and make some friends, the poor, little Mandy had to disappear like that. What a misery for her poor mother.'

While the old lady was busy with her life story, Gwyneth's mind started wondering. Something she always allowed herself to do when she did not feel like handling a situation right then. For no particular reason, she thought of cleaning up the kitchen and giving it a good scrub.

'Please excuse me, Bessie, but I think I'm going to clean up the kitchen a little bit.'

She knew she might have sounded a bit abrupt, but the droning of the old lady's voice actually irritated her. Without saying anything further, she got up and went into the kitchen. The tiny kitchen was scarcely furnished, as was the rest of the house.

It was the enormous deepfreeze that attracted Gwyneth's attention like it did on previous occasions. Strange that a small, old lady, who hardly ate anything, would need such a big deepfreeze, she thought to herself.

More worried about what happened to Mandy and her grieving mother, she started cleaning up. She started cleaning methodically and her mind went back to all the wonderful times her and Mandy spent together.

It was with a shock that she discovered that Mandy was gone. Her mother told her that the police thought that she might have been abducted in the clearing between Bessie's house and the cemetery after her last visit to the old lady.

Gwyneth , however, just knew that Mandy was too responsible a person to be lured into a stranger's car. Whoever did something to her had to be from their own little community. This fact sent a shiver down her spine. She was so convinced of her idea that a killer might be in their midst, that she started feeling quite concerned about her going home later that afternoon.

A quick glance at her watch made her realise that she'd been in the kitchen for almost an hour.

'Bessie,' she called out, 'I think I'm going home a bit earlier today. That is if you don't mind, of course.'

'Of course I don't mind, deary. Best you get going. One wouldn't want anything to happen to another young girl. I'll see you next week then, alright?'

Gwyneth collected all her stuff and decided to make sure that the backdoor was locked. While passing through the kitchen her eye caught the awkwardly big deepfreeze again.

For the first time she noticed the tiny, silvery padlock on the old-fashioned handle of the deepfreeze. What a weird thing to do, she thought, locking a deepfreeze. And with that, such a contrast; the old handle and such a high-tech looking little padlock.

Well, she mused further, old Bessie is most probably going a bit senile.

On her way home, Gwyneth started feeling a bit guilty that she just left Bessie by herself like that. She also realised for the first time that the old lady actually irritated her in a way.

Maybe it was just because of all the strange things going on that I was a bit agitated, she thought. The police investigations still went on for a couple of weeks.

Nothing.

Not a trace of anything to shed light on what might have happened to Mandy. Growing concern for their children made the adults of the village very weary of sudden strangers showing up in their, previously safe little town.

Bessie had also been interrogated a couple of times, but unfortunately was not able to aid the police whatsoever in their investigation. Mandy's mother insisted that the police force from a neighbouring, bigger town be called in to assist their police to find out what had happened to her Mandy. The latter was done but still to no avail.

There was absolutely no trace of the young girl anywhere.

In the meantime life went its normal course. Kids went to school. Their parents to work and Gwyneth to Bessie's on a Saturday. She was contacted by the matron of the old-age home a few weeks ago.

Matron Beechley explained that, although it was a terrible thing that Mandy was missing, they still needed someone to go over to Bessie's house, seeing that she could not cope on her own.

Gwyneth, thanks to Mandy's influence, joined the volunteer group more than a year before and she had to admit to herself that she thoroughly enjoyed it as well.

The past few weeks, however, made her feel less comfortable when she did her weekly round up to Bessie's house. The old lady never seemed to mention Mandy's name anymore and this upset Gwyneth a bit. It was as if Bessie had forgotten about her lost friend already.

Admittedly, Bessie only knew her for a few weeks, but she had the impression that Bessie had no compassion. On the other hand, the old lady was still as friendly as before. This in itself was also upsetting as it felt as if Bessie had forgotten that Mandy has ever been to her house.

With a mind full of turmoil, Gwyneth went to the old house like clockwork every Saturday as expected.

It was the first day of the school vacation and Gwyneth could not wait to go do her last volunteer job. Ever!

The matron already knew and wanted to inform old Bessie. Gwyneth insisted in telling her herself. At last it was Saturday and now she could go and fulfil her 'moral duty,' as she called it.

One last day in the strange old lady's house; telling her that she was leaving, cleaning up for the last time and then … yes, and then what?

She did not know exactly. Maybe she could find a job at the local video store. And get paid! This thought made her feel extremely guilty and two-faced as if she, all of a sudden, needed to be paid for what she did. Knowing that it was not really true, she tried to push all of these thoughts aside. When the time came, she would know what to do with her spare time. Besides, the following year would be her last at school and maybe she should just rather study hard to be able to go study somewhere in a big city.

The way to Bessie's house felt extra long to her as she made her way across the clearing. A strange sensation all of a sudden filled her stomach. Was it excitement, or was there a touch of bad-omen anxiety? She could not tell and as a matter of fact did not care much. She was only a few hours away from, what she felt, freedom.

Not so much freedom from Bessie, but more freedom from the memories of Mandy being lost and the thoughts of her, whenever she went to the house near the cemetery.

'Well,' Gwyneth thought, *'let's make the last day a pleasant one, okay?'*

She reached the old tattered front door and was just about to take out her key when old Bessie opened the door. A bit startled, Gwyneth greeted her with not a lot of enthusiasm.

'Your last day, is it?' the old lady said.

'Yes Bessie. Sorry that I'm leaving on such short notice, but I'm sure that Matron Beechley would find a replacement in no time.'

'I'm sure she would, dear.'

For a second Gwyneth thought there was a touch of sarcasm in the old lady's voice, but then discarded the idea. Bessie had as much emotion as a pork-chop on a barbeque on a Saturday afternoon. Although, the way it was said sort of made her think about Bessie's tone of voice for a while.

She immediately started her weekly routine. Bessie asked her to do the bedroom first as she was not feeling very well and wanted to go lie down for an hour or so.

Gwyneth noticed that the fragile old lady did not look too healthy today. In fact, she looked a bit anaemic to her and totally fatigued.

After a quick rearranging of magazines, etc. she remade the bed and then started tackling the rest of the house.

The last, at last, was the kitchen.

'A fast wipe, dishes, a little sweeping and then I'm off,' she mumbled to herself.

The big, grey cat greeted her as she entered the tiny room. He, or she, was sitting on the big deepfreeze, licking away at a piece of plastic that was sticking out of one of the corners of the enormous casket, normally used to freeze things in.

Gwyneth could not get rid of the idea that it looked like something coming out of a spaceship. Except for the old-fashioned handle, that is. She also noticed that the padlock was undone. Strange indeed, as she always noticed that it was securely locked.

It opened quite easily as she lifted the lid after she had chased the big, grey cat off the freezer. A puff of frozen air rose from the metal box and Gwyneth had to move away half a step.

Reaching out to push the piece of plastic back into the deepfreeze, her eyes fell on something reflected by the kitchen light. Most of the vapour had subsided by then and she recognised the object that was causing the reflection straight away. Her stomach started turning and it was with great difficulty that she kept the late breakfast from that morning from rushing up her throat and spilling onto the floor.

It was Mandy's bracelet that she, Gwyneth, gave her last Christmas.

The fact that it was still around Mandy's arm gave her a feeling of absolute repulsion and she had to swallow again not to vomit all over the contents of the big freezer.

Parts of Mandy was still in the deepfreeze. All packed in plastic bags and labelled in a strange writing. She tried to scream, but she could not even get one sound over her lips.

Everything within her was frozen. Just like the body parts of her dearest friend here in that freezer. Here in the sick old lady's house.

There was no comprehension. No indication of what the consequences might be of her terrible discovery.

Gwyneth wanted to get out of the house, to get away from this dreadful nightmare that was staring her in the face.

But there was only one problem. She just could not move. She was totally paralysed. It was as if she were wearing boots made out of lead.

A shuffle of feet behind her shot a spine-chilling fear into the deepest of her being. *'Don't turn around,'* Gwyneth, her commonsense said to her.

But it was inevitable. She had to see who, or what, it was; a solution or revelation to this unimaginable situation that she was in.

A horrible gurgling sound sent some life into her neck. She very slowly started to turn her head. It just could not be!

Volunteer on Saturdays

The last thing Gwyneth felt was the moisture in her panties as she wet herself with utmost fear and horror…

The disappearance of Gwyneth was known by most of the town's people just after nightfall. When the young girl was not home by sunset, her mother started phoning around frantically to all her friends and then eventually to the police.

Bessie was contacted right away, but she insisted that Gwyneth left her place round three o'clock that afternoon. A search for Gwyneth was immediately instituted and just about everybody joined to go look for her. But to no avail. She had disappeared into thin air by the look of things.

There was a knock on Bessie's door early the Sunday morning. The old lady took some time before answering. She seemed to be extremely tired and her complexion was a dull greyish colour.

After another half an hour of interrogation, she eventually convinced the police that Gwyneth left her house the previous afternoon round three and in very good spirits.

'Could you gentlemen please excuse me now?' she asked after they finished their coffee, 'I am very tired. Didn't sleep too well last night. If there is anything else I could assist you with, please do call.'

With that the police left.

They walked pass the tiny bedroom in the front of the house where the curtains were half-drawn. Nobody bothered to look inside. More important things were on their mind to bother to look into the window of an old lady's bedroom.

If they had bothered to look, they might have seen the three-hundred year old lady taking off her nightgown; revealing leather-like flesh that slightly resembled the bark of a tree.

Nobody saw the naked figure climbing on top of her bed. Nor did anyone see the way she arched her back, like an eighteen year old gymnast, when the first convulsions started.

The hands and feet were moving closer together and eventually merged to form a hideous mass of old, twisted flesh.

What seemed to be feet started growing from the base of this entity. Two arms appeared on either side while the head of the old lady disappeared into this new body as if it were swallowed by the neck.

Where the navel of the human shape used to be, a cone-shaped object started protruding. In a couple of minutes two big, black eyes that made part of this terrifying oblong head, were scanning the room to get adjusted to the light.

It was hungry. Very hungry. And it was time to feed.

The first young human female's body was almost consumed to its full potential. The last girl made her terrible discovery just at the right time.

It needed some more provisions and it had all intentions of eliminating that last one anyway.

It also knew that it could not stay in town for much longer as it became a bit dangerous. Too many questions asked.

When its food was nearing an end it would have to move on. Maybe to a place where the people are less concerned about what was going on around them.

Except for a big, grey cat sitting on a chair in the scarcely furnished bedroom, nobody saw this incredible transformation.
Nobody.

Gemini

A variety of Chinese lanterns illuminated the terraced garden of Coline Heath's enormous mansion in Katherine Street. The neighbours in the Wendywood area knew that it was party-time again. They did not mind much, because most people knew the well-renowned bank manageress and her often flashy lifestyle. Her parties were always done in superb taste and only the cream of the crop got invited.

After the premiere of the latest Hollywood blockbuster, Coline and a few friends stayed for one glass of champagne in the foyer of the Sandton Sun International Hotel. They then headed to her house. She made sure that everything was in order that afternoon before she left to go pick up her friend in Bryanston.

The friend was actually a little more than just that. The two of them had been lovers for almost six years. With an age difference of approximately ten years, Coline thought in the beginning stages of their relationship that things were not going to work out. Fortunately Jedd proved to be rather mature in the situation.

Tonight was a different story, though.

Coline was sitting on the corner of her luxurious double-bed in her spacious and tastefully decorated bedroom. After Jedd's distasteful remark, Coline felt it quite appropriate to reprimand him in front of their guests. This sort of behaviour from Jedd seemed to be happening on a more regular basis and Coline just could not tolerate it any longer. She got up from the bed to pour herself a Chivas Regal from the tiny bar in the one corner of the room.

She was thinking back to what had occurred about ten minutes earlier.

For some time now, their personal, romantic feelings had subsided and were replaced by mere tolerance and acceptance that they were seen as the perfect, though odd, couple. Neither of them frequented the public, single scene, but made no secret of their affection for one another when the situation permitted. Both of them were also prominent figures in the social scene and therefore lived an extremely discreet life, except maybe in the presence of their close friends.

Coline was thinking back to the day six years ago when the young man came to the bank where she was working. At that point in time she was still only the credit manager, thus responsible for personal loans, hire-purchases, etcetera.

JEDD ARMSTRONG was written in big, bold letters on the application form. The young man explained that he was doing modelling as a profession. Coline knew that she was not suppose to grant loans easily to freelance workers. Jeff Armstrong, however, was prepared for her arguments and retrieved a folder from his crocodile skin briefcase and gave it to her in her hands.

It was his modelling portfolio.

Coline went through the references and photographs with more curiosity than really fulfilling her professional duties. It was indeed a matter of love at first sight.

She then decided not to beat about the bush and told Jedd that she could not promise anything, but she would give it a serious consideration. The Provincial Bank that she was working for then, and still was presently, was the sponsor for a new ballet by one of the performing arts councils. Being in a senior position at the bank, she took two tickets from her desk's drawer and handed them to Jedd.

'Here you go, Mr. Armstrong. Should your personal loan application be approved, I would like to assume that you will, being a new client, transfer all your existing bank accounts to us. Here is a little, let's say, welcoming gift.'

With that, Jedd got up and left with a promise to be at the opening of the ballet.

Coline was overjoyed when Jedd showed up that evening at the Civic Centre alone. After the performance, everybody was invited to a cheese-and-wine.

Not long after that, the two newly acquainted persons were entwined in passionate sex in the very same room where Coline Heath was presently standing, sipping her drink with a feeling of utter dismay.

The fact of the matter was that she still cared a lot for her friend. But the whole situation became unbearable the minute Jedd became the model for the new eau de cologne called 'Sauvage.' Stress finally took its toll as he had to work late hours, sometimes seven days a week. His life was filled with promotional work, personal appearances, television shows, modelling shows and photo shoots all over the country.

All these factors started causing problems, not only in their love-life, but also in their normal every day existence. Tonight was the final straw for Coline. She was having a conversation with a good friend, who just happened to be her lawyer, and his wife, when Jedd joined their company. Maybe it was the alcohol, Coline just did not know.

Out of the blue Jedd asked if all of them lived monogamous lives. Everybody, a bit startled at this direct question, looked at each other uneasily. Coline thought that such a peculiar question in the middle of decent conversation was uncalled for.

'Jedd, please! Maybe you should put your glass down and take it easy for a while.'

Jedd, however, just looked at her for a few seconds; he blinked his eyes a couple of times before he replied.

'Well, dear, if you can't answer the question, I suppose there must be a reason. Come on, Coline! A woman? For crying out loud! And that a client of yours? How low can you go?!'

'Jedd!' Coline shouted, 'you're obviously drunk. Rather go home if you can't keep decent conversation.'

'But,' Jedd started, 'I really think …'

He was not given the time to complete his sentence.

'I said go home!' Coline shouted, trembling with rage. Jedd said nothing. With an expression of disgust on his face he threw his glass into the shrubs and rushed toward the driveway where his car was parked.

There was a screeching of tyres as he pulled off into the street. Coline apologised for his friend's conduct. She then excused himself and went into the house; a few minutes to recompose seemed like a good idea.

On the front veranda she stroked the big, grey cat that was lying on one of the garden chairs. With a faint smile and a shake of her head she went up to the bedroom.

'Why on earth would Jedd think I was having something with one of my clients? And a woman at that? It was totally unheard of!'

While this thought was occupying her mind, it dawned on her that she had a client at the bank who had unimaginable financial problems.

The man was impossible to talk to due to his verbal outbursts, so his wife came by a few times to do the talking. Jedd dropped by twice already when she was there.

Then there was the occasion when the woman was in a state of hysterics and she, Coline, decided to take her for a coffee at the quaint little coffee shop on the corner.

Once again Jedd passed by; he even joined them for a coffee. Coline did not think anything of it at that time, but she remembered that she and her client stopped talking about bank business as a matter of professional confidentiality and courtesy.

She supposed that Jedd started getting suspicious. With the stress of his commitments, he must have assumed that she, was being unfaithful. What a preposterous, ignorant and stupid idea! She with a woman?!

The bang of the bedroom door hitting the wall shook Coline out of his thoughts. She swung around to face whoever was entering his bedroom in such a fashion.

It was Jedd. His face was contorted with anger and hatred.

'If you're not here to apologise for your behaviour, you can just as well turn around and leave! And this time, please don't bang the door.'

'You filth!' Jedd shouted, 'always so cool and full of yourself. Well listen to me, missy. Your reign as Queen Almighty has come to an end. Believe me!'

A cigarette was securely placed between his lips and with a flick of his Zippo he lit it with an unsteady hand. He inhaled deeply as he watched Coline intently.

'Jedd, I really don't know what's going on with you. You have become impossible lately and that honestly leaves me with a feeling of total indifference. We don't talk anymore. There's basically nothing between us. But believe me, I still care a lot about you. Maybe we should go up to the cabin for a weekend to try and sort this out with some peace and quiet around us.'

As Jedd replied, smoke was pouring out of his nostrils and mouth.

'You always have an answer, don't you, Queen Bee? Now listen carefully. I am here for a reason. You will most probably not understand, but you have ruined my life, you piece of garbage. I lie awake at night, not able to sleep. You have shattered all dreams, all expectations I've ever had. You have stripped me of all bloody decency and self respect I've had. Thanks to you, I've got nothing at all left in this world and it's all your bloody fault.'

There was something strange about Jedd that Coline could not put her finger on. The fact that he had started smoking again was also a big surprise. As far as she knew, Jedd quit smoking almost a year ago. She realised that they must have drifted apart immensely if she did not even realise that he had taken up smoking again.

'My fault?' Coline asked. 'Dear boy, don't blame others for your inadequacies. I have done nothing but support you all these years. I really don't know what you're talking about. Now if you don't mind, I've got guests waiting.'

She started moving towards the door, but a hard, naked fist collided with her face, consequently breaking her nose. The impact sent her flying across the bedroom floor.

'You're not going anywhere!'

It was Jedd speaking again, but the ringing in Coline's ears made it almost impossible to hear what he was saying. Blood was streaming out of her noise and it hurt profoundly. The young man planted a well-aimed kick in her stomach as she lay on the floor. A gasp of air escaped her lungs as she groaned with indescribable pain.

'Jedd! Stop it! What are you doing?!'

'I told you, sweetheart, it's pay-back time!'

Jedd was now reaching inside his jacket and with horror Coline saw a thin-bladed knife clutched between the white knuckles of the man she used to love so much.

'Jedd, no!' she shouted. 'What are you doing?'

Instinctively Coline knew that she was not going to get an answer. What she did know was that she had to make an attempt to defend herself if she wanted to get out of this nightmare alive. Unfortunately, it was too late.

The first stab went straight into her stomach. A quick withdrawal of the knife caused Coline to scream with pain and horror. The scream was well smothered with Jedd's other hand and he continued stabbing the defenceless woman lying on the bedroom floor.

Blood was squirting out of the wound like a tiny fountain. The young man kept on stabbing his victim until he was sure that there was no life left in this woman that he hated and despised with such intensity that he sometimes could not understand it himself.

After a short while he sat down on the carpet to catch his breath; he got up and went to the bathroom to clean himself up. He had fulfilled his purpose that night and it was time to go home.

He fully intended to leave via the front door. It did not matter to him if anybody saw him. As a matter of fact, he wanted to be seen.

The chief investigator at Brixton Murder and Robbery Squad dropped the file of the previous night's murder on his desk. It was already in the newspapers, though nothing spectacular. Only a small article with no significant information and a photograph of the bank manageress.

Since early that morning a lot of witnesses, who attended the party, had been questioned and now it was time to go visit super model, Mr. Jedd Armstrong, at his house in Bryanston. Chief Denny hated visiting these snobbish areas, but in this case decided to do the interrogation himself. As he was driving up Corlett Drive whilst looking for the house number, he hoped that this case would be wrapped up very quickly. The reporters would be swarming the scene of the murder soon and at the police station they had to be prepared for hundreds of phone calls before lunch time. That was a definite fact.

    The gate leading up to the enormous house opened without any noise after he announced himself over the intercom. Jedd answered the buzz from the pool where he was doing his morning laps. This was a daily routine, even after a party the previous evening. He informed the chief via the intercom that the front door would be open and that he had to go through to the lounge.

    Entering the big lounge, the inspector was quite impressed with the expensive, yet excellent taste, in which it was decorated. His attention was immediately drawn to the only painting against the cream-coloured wall. It was a uniquely painted landscape with an old farm house and surrounding trees. The cumulus clouds that hovered in the sky gave it a magnificent finishing touch.

'It's a genuine Pierneef, you know.'

The inspector turned around by the friendly voice and stared at a young man in his mid-thirties, drying his hair with a towel. Dressed only in a bright blue Speedo, the inspector was amazed at how good-looking this Adonis was. A perfect build with athletic legs and a muscled chest created the image of something that was only to be found in a fashion magazine. Realising that he was actually staring at the skimpily dressed young man made him look away rather embarrassed.

Jedd noticed the man's embarrassment and felt a bit flattered knowing that another man was admiring his physique, even if it were only for a fleeting moment.

'Jedd Armstong,' he introduced himself.

'I know,' Inspector Denny answered, 'I am Chief Investigator Denny. I am sure you know why I am here.'

'Well, yes … eh, what shall I call you? ' Jedd asked.

'Inspector will suffice.'

'Well, Inspector, I do know why you are here. But please make yourself comfortable. I have to go take a quick shower. Pour yourself a drink in the meantime. I won't be too long.'

He wrapped the towel around his waist and started for the stairs in the corner of the lounge, situated adjacent to the sliding doors where he had just entered.

'Do you have any mineral water?' Inspector Denny asked, 'can't take any alcohol, sorry. Sugar diabetes. Thank you for offering just the same.'

'Of course. In the fridge behind the bar counter. Inspector, relax. I am only going to be a few minutes. If you don't trust me, you can always come and keep an eye on me, you know.'

Jedd said this with a twinkle in his eyes, just to cause the inspector a bit more embarrassment. Inspector Denny was annoyed by this last remark and the behaviour of the young man, but decided not to get intimidated by it at all. Armstrong had his time of being in charge as far as he was concerned. Soon the inspector would really have Armstrong by the short and curlys, figuratively speaking, of course.

While waiting for the young man to return, Inspector Denny could not help but wondering why he was so calm about the whole affair. He seemed to be very relaxed with not so much as a trace of being nervous or worried. Was Armstrong that cold blooded, or was there something else about the situation that he, Denny, did not know about? He supposed that a lot would come out once Armstrong returned to the lounge and he could ask him a couple of questions.

Somehow the whole concept of Armstrong's behaviour seemed to induce some doubt in the mind of the inspector. This was going to be an open and shut case, he had said to himself that morning before he left the station.

But now something was nibbling at the corners of his intuition. Thanks to years of experience he came to realise within minutes when someone was putting on an act and was indeed guilty of a crime or not. This Armstrong baffled him so much that he decided to question all the guests from the party to obtain the finest details of the happenings from the previous evening.

There was something wrong and he knew it.

He gave a sigh and took a Daonil from the small plastic container in his pocket; part of his daily ritual, repeated three times, it became such a habit that he did not even realise that he was doing it anymore.

Jedd appeared on the staircase about fifteen minutes later; dressed in a beige linen shirt and shorts with comfortable sailor shoes, he poured himself a diet Coke and sat down in a chair opposite the inspector.

'Now, tell me,' Jedd said smilingly, 'am I a suspect in the murder of my … uh … my lover? Or should I say ex-lover, hm?'

'Yes, Mr. Armstrong, you are indeed a suspect. As a matter of fact, the only suspect at the moment. See, we have eye-witnesses who saw you entering the house and they also saw you leaving after a couple of minutes. Shortly after that Miss. Heath's body was discovered by a friend. Now, what do you have to say about that, hm?'

Jedd suddenly realised that there was a rat in the kitchen. He could not believe what the inspector just told him. He got up and started pacing the room.

'Inspector Denny, please believe me that, after I had an argument with Coline, I left the property and I haven't been back since.'

Inspector Denny looked at him without saying anything for a few minutes. Then he asked Jedd if it was in order if he smoked in the house. Jedd nodded affirmatively and went to the lounge to fetch an ashtray. On his return he was offered a Camel, but politely refused.

'I quit smoking eleven months ago, thanks. Now doesn't seem like a bad time to start again, does it? This just doesn't make sense. Honestly!'

Inspector Denny noticed that the sarcasm and tease in the man's voice were replaced with insecurity and perhaps a little bit of fear. He decided to give Jedd the opportunity to tell him what exactly happened the previous night.

'Mr. Armstrong,' Inspector Denny implored, 'why don't you tell me what happened last night? Or maybe I should say this morning, rather?'

Jedd started relating to the inspector about his jealous suspicions that Coline was having an affair with someone. In the fashion industry was a lot of gossip and strife and it was not always easy to keep one's problems to oneself. He explained that he trusted a colleague with his personal problems and that caused him to start doubting Coline's fidelity. Many ridiculous ideas were put into his head and he started believing them. It has always been one of his philosophies in life, where there was smoke, there was fire!

Jedd described the evening to the inspector with utmost precision as if he had to make sure that Denny believed him right there and then. It was as if he was thinking that he would not get another chance to explain what happened.

With detailed and vivid images Jedd told the Inspector about the première of the movie, the champagne afterwards and about their argument in the car on the way to the house in Wendywood. After heavy drinking at the fancy party, a subsequent fall-out was inevitable.

Jedd said that he was immensely infuriated and felt that he had to leave before the situation got out of hand. The solitude of his own house did not seem very appealing and he decided at the spur of the moment to go to the sauna.

'You know the one up in Grayston Drive, Inspector?'

The big chief investigator felt that Jedd's last question was more a rhetorical question, so he did not answer, but indicated by shaking his head that he did not know the sauna.

It did not take long for Jedd to tell the course of events to the inspector.

By now his voice was trembling as he said to Inspector Denny, 'I don't know who came to the house last night, but believe me, it sure as hell wasn't me.'

Inspector Denny left the mansion in Bryanston with a lot of mixed emotions. That morning he was totally convinced that the male model had killed his own, somewhat older lover. Driving back to the station that feeling that he was once again correct in his judgement, had subsided quite a bit.

Exactly why he felt that way, he could not say. But for one thing he was certain of, Jedd Armstrong did not smoke. Neither did Coline Heath. But a cigarette bud was found squashed on the carpet in the bedroom of the dead woman. It was not crushed by a shoe, but it appeared rather that someone rolled over it, hence crushing it. It had to be when the deceased and the killer were having a fight.

A DNA test should reveal if it was actually smoked by Jedd Armstrong. This case needed a lot more investigation.

The head-lines in the newspapers all over the country had more-or-less the same message. One of the leading papers put it in a simple, but striking manner:

MALE MODEL KILLS SUGAR MOMMY!

Jedd Armstrong was found guilty of murder in the first degree. The judge's ruling was predominantly made due to the testimonies of the eye-witnesses and a positive result of the DNA test that indicated that the DNA found on the cigarette but belonged to the accused.

The young, well-known man was seen having an argument with his lover. He then left in a rage to return less than thirty minutes later and with an obvious intense fury ran into the house. Shortly after, he returned outdoors again and left with the awaiting taxi. The driver of the taxi also identified Jedd at a later stage as one of his customers that night.

Jedd Armstrong was sentenced to life imprisonment. All of this was a huge shock to the fashion industry as well as to the general public.

Inspector Denny knew that the concern would make way for total disinterest within a couple of weeks. Jedd's lawyer was filing for appeal, but the policeman had an idea that the court was convinced that he was guilty.

Chief Investigator Denny, however, was convinced otherwise.

A few months prior to the brutal murder of the bank manageress, Coline Heath, another man in his mid-thirties was sitting at the dentist's consulting rooms in Sandton City; an enormous shopping centre in the northern suburbs that not only supplied executive stores and supermarkets, but also tended to the needs of people in search of the skills of lawyers, doctors, accountants and in the case of this other man, Rubin Jacobs, a dentist.

He was an angry man. Not only because of the pain one of his maulers had been causing him, but he was just in general an angry man. The type who never had any luck in life and therefore blamed everything on society.

He was totally consumed in his own thoughts and did not care one bit of what was going on around him. His wife was seeing someone behind his back. That he was convinced about. To make things worse, it was not a man. If it were a man, at least he would have been able to do something about it. No, Rubin Jacobs believed that his wife was getting involved with a woman. And not just any woman; no, the woman who had been ruining his life as far as he was concerned.

The past few years had been very difficult for him. Everything he turned his hand to seemed to turn to dust.

His latest development just had to be a huge success; Rubin was convinced of that. All his savings and all their vacation money were put into the project. He even sold his car and bought a small, second-hand piece of scrap to get around with. To manufacture his patented idea, however, was still going to cost thousands.

Then he was informed by the prissy bank manageress that her bank was not prepared to assist. Not even a second bond on the house, never mind a personal loan.

All production had stopped and he had fallen into a rut. Depression got the better of him.

The fact that the witch at the bank had blocked all doors, even at other financial institutions, increased his anger and hatred.

He was a financial risk, according to the bank.

How he hated that Miss Coline Heath.

After several private visits to the bank herself, his wife had started denying him the carnal pleasures of life all of a sudden. He was convinced she was having an affair.

The magazines lying on the little table attracted Rubin's attention.

Why do they always put all these girly magazines out at the doctor's?

He nevertheless picked up a Cosmopolitan and started paging through it. Although he was not really paying attention as he flipped through the pages, his whole world came to a halt as his eyes fell upon the face of the man in red spandex shorts with a small bottle of perfume held provocatively with one hand in front him.

Immediately Rubin's mind went back to his sixteenth birthday as his hand caressed the beard that he had grown the passed few months. Oh, how well did he remember the day his parents told him that he was adopted and his real birthday was on the thirtieth of May.

He smiled as he touched his face and took off his glasses.

The diabolical plan started developing right there and then in his evil mind.

A hair cut, a shave and a few minutes without his glasses should do it, he smiled.

Rubin had no knowledge of the relationship between Jedd Armstrong and Coline Heath at that point in time. That, of course, did not matter. He was going to commit the perfect murder, with the help of the model's face in the magazine.

Without as much as a glance at the receptionist, he tore the page out.

The name of the male model as well as the name of the modelling agency were at the bottom of the page. He knew it would take some time and especially proper surveillance of the guy in the magazine, but all-in-all it was going to be a piece of cake.

'You are going to pay, my Queen Bee,' he whispered under his breath, 'you're going to pay big time!'

The receptionist called out his name and indicated that he would be next. The toothache seemed to have disappeared and was replaced by an evil, yet satisfying grimace on his face.

Gemini

He was glad, very impressed as a matter of fact, that he was a Gemini in more ways than one.

Rachel

The sun just started peeping through the clouds and utmost delight came to Rachel's heart. Today was Saturday and it was her birthday. She was very happy that the sun was going to shine, because earlier that morning, while she was still washing the breakfast dishes, she thought it was going to be a miserable day. There was a grey sky and for a few minutes it looked like snow. But now that the rays of the sun started pushing the grey clouds away, she just knew that her tenth birthday was going to be most memorable.

It was the year 1835. Rachel and her family; that was Father, Mother and her younger brother of four years, Jonathan, had moved to this foreign country about five years earlier. They were part of the first Settlers to move to a new, sunny country in the South. They left a cold, rainy country behind them. In the beginning all of them were quite scared, though rather excited, about discovering the new frontiers, but all in all it was still an unknown future awaiting them.

Although Rachel was only five years at the time when they embarked on their sea voyage, she remembered vividly the evening when Father came home, after a long discussion with some executives in the city.

'Mother, Rachel, I have some exciting news!' he exclaimed as he opened the front door of their little house. He was all smiles and Rachel and Mother knew that it had to be something terrific.

What is it dear?' asked Mother, as she gave him a good evening kiss and embraced him lovingly, as she always did.

'We're going to move, my darlings,' he said, equally excited as a little boy who was getting a present for his birthday.

'Oh, Father,' cried Mother, 'are we moving to the countryside, as we've always wanted?'

Father just smiled and explained that, not only were they going to move to the countryside, but to another, warm country in the South altogether.

All of them were very excited. Over the weeks that followed, everybody was busy with arrangements, packing, saying goodbye to family and friends and just getting anxious as the time neared for them to depart. On their last evening, they had a grand party at home. All their friends and family were invited.

    Rachel smiled as she recalled the long journey by ship. Weeks it took them, but when they finally got to shore, it was a beautiful, sunny day and they were all convinced that they would be happy in their new country. Father was allocated a small farm that they could live on, but the cooperation also gave him a job as a part time clerk; the same work that he used to do before they moved there.

    A year or so later little Jonathan was born, much to the joy of not only Mother and Father, but also to Rachel. She was happy that she would have a little brother to play with; look after and be friends with. For even though she attended the local farm school and was befriended with the other children there and youngsters in the neighbourhood, it would have been nice to have another child for company at home.

    Time had passed by quickly for all of them and, before they realized it, it was already Rachel's tenth birthday.

    Their new country was a splendid place. There was sunshine almost all year round. They loved their little farm which was their new home. After being on the farm for only a few days, they decided to call it 'Ant Hill Farm,' as there were a lot of ant hills on their grounds. As a matter of fact, there were hundreds of ant hills in the vicinity; some small, some a bit bigger and some of them so high, that Rachel had to stand on her tiptoes to be able to see right over them.

Sometimes, when she had finished her chores in the afternoon, she would take Jonathan by the hand and go exploring. Of course, always under the guiding eye of Mother, who would watch them as they went about the back part of the big yard, looking for all sorts of treasures and interesting things. The back yard wasn't really a yard as such, but more an open, flat field that stretched out all the way to the foot of the mountain.

Rachel and Jonathan were never allowed to go all the way up to where the mountain started. Both Mother and Father warned them never to go into the mountain area.

'I wouldn't want my babies to get lost in the trees and the rocks and the anthills, now would I?' Mother always said.

Rachel always solemnly promised never to venture out that far and she always kept her word. She was a very pleasant girl with a good disposition. All the people from the surrounding farms grew to love Rachel. She always had time to stop for a quick chat with everybody on her way to school. She also excelled as a good student and every day Rachel took a little surprise for her teacher. If it was not a bouquet of wild flowers that she picked on her way to the little farm school, it was an apple, or a basket full of ripe tomatoes and sometimes, when it was the season, she would even take a small pumpkin to school, much to her teacher's delight.

Over the years Father had established a nice home for him and his family. Even though he had a regular job at the cooperation, he took care of Ant Hill Farm with the skill of an experienced farmer. They only had a few animals on the farm; a few sheep, a milk cow and a couple of goats.

He built a huge paddock on the far side of the huge yard and a little barn with three wooden walls for shelter for the animals in this paddock. Around the barn, there was a small encampment. So basically there was a small paddock within the big paddock. The smaller paddock's fence consisted of a wooden fence and a strong gate, which could be shut at night, just in case some jackal; wild boar or other wild predators roamed the area.

Mother milked the cow every morning, but Father took it on himself to do the milking in the evenings and over the weekends. They had to keep the animals in a paddock, otherwise they would wander off into the wilderness of the mountain, but the paddock was quite spacious with lots of room to run and walk and lie down, whenever the animals felt like it.

During the Winter months it got quite cold where they lived. In the midst of Winter it even snowed.

But the family was quite content, even when it snowed. In the old country, it was forever raining and when Winter came, it was immensely cold and it snowed almost every day. So, in the new place, they did not mind the snow, as it was only for a week or two in Winter. Before the sun set, all the animals were locked in, safe and sound.

It was almost lunch time and Rachel knew that they were going to have a very special lunch for her birthday. She was allowed to invite a few friends. Knowing that they would start arriving in a couple of minutes, Rachel was getting ready to receive her friends when they got there.

She was alone in her bedroom; putting on her prettiest Sunday dress that Mother had made for her a few weeks before. She really loved her dress. It was made out of unbleached linen and it had three layers. The dress was rather plain, but it reached almost down to her ankles, just the way she liked it. To add some colour, Mother made a full-length apron-like overdress in a light blue material. The borders were stitched with old lace from a curtain that Mother did not use anymore.

As it was cold outside, they would have her birthday party in the big kitchen and living room, which Rachel helped to decorate during the course of the morning.

She put on her long, woollen socks and then her short ankle-boots, which she cleaned and polished the previous night before she went to bed.

Rachel had a look in the mirror and realized that something was missing. Quickly she grabbed her brush and gave her hair ten vigorous strokes. Then she took a ribbon, made from the same light blue material as her overdress. Carefully lifting her shiny, shoulder-length brown hair, she put the ribbon underneath her hair at the back and tied a beautiful bow on top of her head. She then picked a small branch of dainty white flowers that Mother had put in the vase on her night stand that morning. She carefully stuck the flowers in her hair, just above her right ear. Now she was ready to welcome her guests.

Rachel just walked out of her bedroom, when Mother called.

'Rachel, dear, I think some of your friends have just arrived in a buggy!'

Everybody had a splendid time. Rachel was overwhelmed with all the felicitations, good wishes and presents. Everybody enjoyed the hot chocolate that was offered to them on arrival. After a small lunch, all the youngsters went to play some games in the living room. At about three o'clock, Mother and Father came into the room where all the youngsters were sitting on the floor.

Rachel was telling them about their life they had in their old country. They were all virtually hanging on Rachel's lips and were quite intrigued by her narration. Mother softly interrupted.

'Darling, round up your story, because we have a surprise for everyone in the kitchen.' That was more than enough inspiration for Rachel to end her story, but she was sure to end it quite dramatically.

Afterwards they all rushed into the kitchen. There, on the then empty kitchen table, was the biggest, most decorative chocolate birthday cake that Rachel, and her friends, for that matter, had ever seen.

'Oh, Mother,' she cried, 'it is beautiful!'

As the others also shouted their ooh's and aah's, Rachel got tears in her eyes. Oh, how she loved her parents for making such a beautiful birthday possible for her.

The cake was rectangle in shape and her name was written with pink icing in very artistic letters.

Underneath her name were ten candles in the shape of the number 10. They were all lit and, as it was getting dark because of the grey weather that started up again during the afternoon, it caused a warm glow, together with the fire in the open kitchen fireplace. It was just too beautiful to describe.

Right at the bottom part of the cake, were a few strange-looking pink blobs of icing. As Rachel went a bit closer to see what they were, she felt somebody pulling at her dress. It was little Jonathan.

'I made flowers for Rachey,' he said, pointing proudly at the pink blobs; he always called her 'Rachey,' as he could never pronounce 'Rachel' properly. Everybody had a good chuckle.

After a wonderful afternoon, everybody left and Mother, Father and Rachel started cleaning up. Even little Jonathan contributed by eating the leftovers in some of the plates.

Everything was cleaned, washed and packed away in no time. Mother and Father informed their two children that they were going to take a little nap. Rachel and Jonathan decided to laze around in the living room, as they were not tired enough to go for a lie down.

They paged through a book that Rachel got from the Vicar's son. There were many picture in it and Rachel started reading the story out loud, so that Jonathan could also enjoy her present.

It was getting quite dark outside when Rachel said, 'Jonathan, go see if Mother and Father are still sleeping, would you?' Jonathan obeyed and a minute later he was back.

'They sleep,' he informed Rachel.

'Well,' said Rachel, 'seeing that they worked so hard to give me such a perfect birthday and I got all these wonderful presents, I'll go and get all the animals to go into the barn.'

'I go too, Rachey,' nagged Jonathan. Rachel thought it over for a minute.

'Oh, alright,' she said, 'but you have to get dressed warmly. It is snowing again and it's freezing out there.'

'Okay, Rachey,' agreed her little brother, 'I put my hat and gloves on.'

'And your warm coat too. There's a good boy.'

Having lived on a farm for so long, Rachel knew exactly how to round up the animals. She also knew that they had to be dressed very warmly, as it was very cold in Winter. Quite the expert, she lit the storm lantern to take with them.

She imagined that Mother and Father must have fallen asleep and that they had not realised it was so late already. But, out of the kindness of her heart, she decided that she would surprise them by getting all the animals into the barn. They would be very proud of her, she thought.

So, off the two went, all warmly wrapped in and with the storm lantern in her hand. It was getting darker very fast by then and Rachel was glad that she took the lantern with them.

By the time they got to the paddock, it was snowing hard and a terrible, icy wind was blowing. Even though they had the lantern with them, they had difficulty to see where they were going in the blizzard.

As Rachel opened the gate of the paddock, one of the little sheep, that was quite frightened because of the storm, jump right over Rachel's leg that she had put in between the gate and the post of the fence to prevent the animals from getting out.

It was too late! The little sheep had escaped and started running like the wind.

'Get him! Get him!' shouted Rachel to Jonathan, as she quickly closed the gate again.

Jonathan started running after the sheep and Rachel started running after Jonathan. The little sheep headed straight for the trees and bushes which grew at the foot of the mountain.

Rachel's mind worked overtime. She knew that they should not go all the way out there, but she also did not want to leave the poor sheep exposed to the cold like that either.

'Jonathan,' she called out, 'you go home and call Father, while I try to find the sheep.'

'No,' cried Jonathan, 'I too scare!'

'It's alright. I'll wait here until you get to the house, then I'll only go after the sheep.'

But before Rachel could get Jonathan to obey her orders, he saw the little sheep moving in the nearby bushes and shouted 'Seep! Seep! There! Over there!' and he rushed off again.

Although he could not run that fast, Rachel had difficulty going after him with the lamp in her hand. And then she tripped over a big stone and fell.

The lantern's flame went out and she could not see Jonathan anymore. She called out to him and started running blindly into the direction where she saw him last. But to no avail.

Jonathan was lost.

She kept on walking around, calling out his name. For how long this went on, she did not know, but, all of a sudden, she heard the bleating of a sheep. Immediately she started moving in the direction of the sound and after a few minutes, she could distinguish the shape of something that was moving in the darkness. It was Jonathan, holding tightly onto the sheep.

'Jonathan!' cried Rachel, 'thank goodness you're safe!'

Jonathan was so glad to hear his sister's voice, that he let go of the sheep and made his way to Rachel. The scared sheep ran off again, leaving the two children all by themselves in the cold, dark, snowy night.

Rachel knew that they were lost and she was very, very frightened.

'Come on, Jonathan, we have to find the house,' she said with a tremor in her voice.

They searched for a long time, but, without knowing it, just walked around in circles.

They were totally and utterly lost.

In the meantime, the little lost sheep had found his way back home and was bleating by the paddock gate. Mother and Father were already up after their nap. At first they thought the children were sleeping, but soon realised that it was not the case.

They started walking around, first in the house and on the veranda, calling their names, but soon spread out into the big back yard, yelling their names at the top of their lungs.

Father eventually took another storm lantern and went outside again. They had been searching for almost an hour, when suddenly they heard the cries of the little sheep. Both Mother and Father ran to the paddock and immediately comprehended what must have happened.

'Mother,' take the mare and go to the neighbours. Tell them that Rachel and Jonathan are lost in the snowstorm.'

Mother first hesitated a bit, as the storm was quite severe and she would rather take the buggy. But she realized that there was no time to be wasted; their children were in danger.

'Alright,' she agreed, 'but put all the storm lanterns out, all the way to the foot of the mountain. This way we'd be able to see the path you took and you'd be able to find your way back again.'

Father agreed and off he went, after fetching some more lanterns in the house, to go find his lost children. Mother saddled the horse as quickly as she could and went off on a light trot into the darkness to the neighbour's farmhouse.

The news of the disappearance of Rachel and Jonathan spread very fast and soon everybody from the neighbouring farms came over to help search for the children. They searched right through the night, but just before dawn, they all agreed to wait until sunrise.

The storm had only subsided during the early hours of the morning. When dawn broke and after having only about an hour or so of rest, everybody got up, had a cup of coffee and some sandwiches, that Mother prepared, and off they went again.

Father was extremely fatigued as he was riding his horse, scanning the area as he went. It was becoming light in the east and he could see a bit better. Then suddenly, he thought that he saw a movement behind some bushes in the distance. It looked like Rachel in her party dress.

'Rachel! Rachel!' he called out eagerly and slightly kicked the horse in the flanks to move forward. As he got closer to what he thought was his daughter, he was convinced that it was indeed Rachel running away from him.

'Rachel, wait!' he shouted and made his horse go into a light canter, but somehow the figure managed to stay a few feet ahead of him. Even when he went into a gallop, the figure of a girl dressed in linen with a light blue apron over-dress kept on running through the bushes, further and further away.

Then suddenly the figure disappeared behind a huge anthill.

Was it his imagination? Was his eyes playing tricks on him? Maybe he was hallucinating because of his tiredness?

At first he did not, or maybe I should say could not, believe what he saw; but, with tears streaming down his face, he came to realise what a wonderful, loving daughter he had.

He found a huge anthill, hollowed out on one side. Rachel's back was sticking out of the hole. She was only dressed in her petticoat. Father lifted her carefully from the hollowed-out anthill. She was totally frozen and ice-cold. Her whole little body was stiff and a pale, purplish colour. It was then when he heard Jonathan cry. After lying Rachel's body carefully on the ground, he saw Jonathan on the inside of the hole in the anthill.

He was alive! Warmly wrapped in his sister's party dress, the light blue overdress and her warm coat. Jonathan was also wearing her gloves and sheepskin hat. Rachel made sure that her brother was safe in the hole and warmly wrapped in. Being the unselfish little girl that she was, she wanted to protect her brother as best she could. Rachel gave her own life to save that of her dear little brother.

On her tenth birthday, Rachel gave a gift herself. The gift of life and the directions to find Jonathan, even though her own life was already gone.

Anna's Child

A warm, blinding winter sun was trying its utmost to penetrate the little wooden hut which was enfolded in a shroud of tranquillity on the hillside leading down into the valley. Everything was covered in the purest snow ever imaginable. Exactly the way Anna liked it.

She was busy preparing a little breakfast for herself and treasured the morning quiet as she was going about her normal morning routine.

'Not time to let the sun in yet,' she said to herself. Still a bit of privacy and then she would be able to allow the outside into her little kingdom.

For the umpteenth time she realised how much she liked her little hut here in Litzirüti, situated on the hillside.

Approximately one kilometre from the roadside, the hut overlooked the tremendous valley with all its slopes and trees that grew all the way down to the bottom. The mountain on the opposite side was just as impressive as the one on her side of the valley. When she opened her backdoor in the mornings, she could always appreciate the greatness of this giant that started escalating directly after the break that the small main road caused in this magnificent part of the world.

The tiny village of Litzirüti was more or less twenty-five kilometres from the city of Chur. Anna was wondering when was the last time that she actually took the train down the mountain to the city. She could not really remember. As a matter of fact, she preferred not to go to a big city at all.

At times, when she needed something important and she could not find it at the village's local store, she would take a slow walk up the mountain to go do her shopping in Arosa. She found the five kilometre walk quite pleasant and usually made a whole outing of it.

The articles and short stories that she wrote for the local newspaper of Arosa were normally given to the storekeeper, who went up to Arosa on a daily basis; he would then hand them in at the office whenever they were completed.

Shortly after she moved here, she invested in an electric typewriter; fortunately there was electricity in the hut. After years of living and working in München, she had managed to save up a lot of money and thus came to live here in Switzerland, shortly after her misfortune a few years ago.

It was with utmost reluctance that her mind went back to her thirtieth birthday.

Her friends still teased her that she was hitting the big 30. A special evening was organised for her and after a wonderful evening of wining and dining in the city centre, they all decided to go dance away all the calories in a nightclub.

It was here that she had met *HIM*. She never even asked what *HIM* was called. Surely he must have introduced himself through the course of the night, but she always used to refer to him afterwards as merely *HIM*, seeing that she could not remember his name.

It was an evening of pure bliss as they made love until the sun came up. As much as she treasured those moments of physical pleasure and emotional intensity, she still recalled with horror what happened afterwards.

The fact that she fell pregnant because of the handsome stranger did not bother her in itself. As a matter of fact, she was overjoyed. No responsibilities to anyone except herself and the little one who was growing inside of her.

Then the whole dream came crushing down. A miscarriage at seven weeks, only a few weeks after she was informed that she was pregnant, left her totally devastated and absolutely empty. With vivid images and emotions she could still remember the pain, the blood and the horror of it all.

Her friends were so supportive, but nothing could substitute the feeling that a part of her life was torn from her body and it would never be replaced.

It was with a friend that she came over here for a week to recover and she immediately fell in love with the area. Her resignation was handed in after her return to work and a few weeks later she moved into her wooden hut; the latter purchased from a retired couple via a telephonic transaction. They had decided to move into an old-age home.

Priority number one was the typewriter.

She did not want to go work in an office again and seeing that she had worked for a publisher in München, she decided to apply her skills in the privacy of her hut.

At first she just wrote insignificant pieces regarding the area and tried to sell them to the local paper. Her talent was spotted immediately and the initial assignments by the paper soon turned into her working full-time as a journalist for the paper. Nothing extreme, but she enjoyed what she was doing.

Approximately two years before she bought her own personal computer and straight away started writing a novel for children. Much time and effort were put into this work. For Anna it was like nurturing a child and not just writing some nonsense that she could eventually make same money with.

A sudden meow from the backdoor shook her out of her thoughts.

'Poor thing,' she sympathised.

It was the stray cat that wanted to come inside. Anna's only real companion for quite some time. She opened the back door to let him in.

'*Another "him",*' she smiled silently.

'I really have a problem putting a name to a face,' she mused, this time out loud in the stillness of the cabin.

The cat's bowl seemed to be missing as Anna looked around in the kitchen. The kitchen was actually situated in one corner of the hut, as was the lounge in the other corner and her bedroom in the third. A small partition cornered off the bathroom area.

As she reached for a clean bowl on the cupboard above the stove, she accidentally dragged a plate underneath it with the bowl. The plate came down with an enormous speed and it landed on her foot with such a force that tears sprang to her eyes instantaneously.

The cat decided that it was much safer underneath the table and was in his place of safety in a second.

'Scheisse!' Anna exclaimed.

The throbbing set in immediately. She tried to ignore the pain and started dishing up some food for the big, grey cat.

Miraculously the plate was not broken and she just put it on top of the stove. She was thinking that maybe she should put some cream or lotion on her foot before it started swelling up.

On her way to the small bathroom in the corner she all of a sudden realised that a strange, chanting kind of noise was coming from outside. Or maybe it was a high-pitched wining from an animal that was hurt. With a very sore foot she went to the door to go have a look.

The tiny bundled-up baby did not make her yell out in surprise. There was not a gasp or anything likewise. Just absolute peace and an intense feeling of pure love.

Anna picked up the infant and had a quick look around if there was anyone in the vicinity. But there was nobody. She did not notice at all that there were no footprints in the snow; none at all around the house or in the little footpath, which was clearly marked with green painted poles leading to the main road. There was a sensation of immense tranquillity as she was holding the baby with utmost care.

'This just can not be!' she exclaimed, 'what am I going to do?'

One thing was for sure: this baby was there for a purpose; she knew that instinctively. And nobody was going to take this bundle of joy, a concept that was only natural to her, away from her. Maybe it was the proper thing to inform the right authorities, but Anna knew that she could not and would not do that. This baby was hers!

But what am I to do? she questioned herself.

'Just say that I am the son of a relative who passed away.'

The thought jumped into her head and with surprise she realised that she did not even know whether it was a boy or a girl.

She unwrapped the baby, which was an unnecessary process, because she knew already that it was a boy. She just knew.

All of a sudden she remembered that the thought that came to her was in the first person.

Strange.

It was as if the idea was spoken into her head by the child himself.

With a shake of her head she discarded the silly idea and started looking for something to make the baby lie down in. The sudden thought that she had a nativity in her stable, adjacent to the hut, from last Christmas, made her go to the stable in a flash.

There it was. A little wooden crib just perfect for her baby.

In no time it was cleaned and nicely arranged with linen and blankets to make the child comfortable and to keep him warm.

While she was busy with the crib, Anna, by then totally lost in thought, had a fleeting feeling that there was something out of the ordinary ever since she had picked up the little baby boy.

The realisation that her foot did not hurt at all anymore only dawned on her when she went up the road a little later to go buy some milk and baby food for her 'cousin from Salzburg's' baby.

Everybody in the neighbourhood knew Anna and nobody hesitated for a moment to believe that she was now the official mother of her cousin's baby, seeing that the cousin died in an unfortunate car accident. Anna was her only living relative and also the godmother of little Luke.

This name was chosen with great care by Anna. It was absolute 'glück', or 'luck', that the baby was left on her doorstep.

More fortune, luck and happiness were nowhere else to be found like those in the heart of Anna. The name 'Luke' was the closest she could come to express what she felt.

Since the child had entered her life, she had been so ecstatic in everything she did; in conversations with others, her work and her book that was coming along nicely. For the first time in years she went to bed at night feeling totally fulfilled.

There was subsequently a lot of visitors each day at the little wooden hut. Normally Anna would not like to be bothered too much in her little kingdom, but she found all the visitations quite pleasant.

It was after a few weeks that she caught herself thinking how everybody left her hut in good cheer and always with a smile on their faces.

The days and weeks had passed and Anna carried on with her weekly articles and she also started spending all her free time with her book. An ex-colleague in München was prepared to do the illustrations for her book, should it eventually go for publishing.

She realised how much easier it was to come up with new ideas. Luke was a very good baby and she never had any problems with him at all.

This in itself brought the realisation to mind that something might be wrong. He never cried, never got sick, slept when he was supposed to and ate very well for such a small baby. With a sudden impulse Anna got up to take him for a full check-up and prepared for the short walk to Doctor Einfeld's rooms.

The old doctor, who also acted as unofficial paediatrician, assured Anna that the boy was in perfect health. Immensely relieved, she relaxed and started to inquire about Frau Einfeld, the doctor's wife.

It was quite a shock when she found out that the old lady was lying in the local hospital with a malignant brain tumour that could not be cured.

She had not been to the doctor since the first time she brought Luke in for a check-up, which was the very day after she had found him on her doorstep.

Since then, she had not been to the doctor at all. As a matter of fact, she herself had never felt so healthy in her whole life. The headaches that used to bother her after working long hours in front of the computer seemed to have ceased altogether as well.

After a quick goodbye, Anna took her baby boy and headed for the community hospital, five blocks up the road.

Frau Einfeld hardly recognised her as she stood at the end of the bed with a bunch of flowers that she bought at the entrance of the building. After a few minutes, some recognition entered the fatigued eyes and a slight smile turned the corners of the cracked lips slightly upwards.

Anna did not really know what to say.

All she felt was utter dismay as she looked at the withering figure of the doctor's dear wife.

Luke was relocated onto her left hip as she reached out to take the sick woman's hand. She gave it a light squeeze, but their was almost no response.

The old lady's eyes were fixated on the little human being on Anna's hip.

With immense effort the old woman lifted her hands, indicating that she would like to take Luke into her arms.

Anna hesitated for a moment, but then handed the baby over with tears in her eyes.

This time there was a definite smile on the old, wrinkled face. One single tear slid down her left cheek. A feeling of sublime peace came over both the women and Anna knew that the old lady was crying with heavenly bliss and not with earthly pain or unhappiness.

Anna went home with a feeling that made her a bit uneasy. It was not as much the visit to the hospital, inasmuch the feeling of urgency that she had now for a couple of days already.

A quick dinner had to suffice that night and afterwards she worked on her book until early hours of the morning. There was a sudden urge to complete this book that she had been working on for so long, that she just could not comprehend.

A lot of time, thought and even some research had been put into her book and a sudden rush to finish it would be catastrophic. Nevertheless, she carried on with an assurance and ease that did not influence her creativity and dedication.

The news of Frau Einfeld's remarkable recovery sent a chill up her spine and left her utterly speechless as she sat down with a touch of fear in her heart.

Martine, the shopkeeper's daughter came to her with the news. The old lady had to go for a brain scan the day after Anna had visited her. There was no chance of recovery from the tumour and yet the scan made it very clear that the tumour was diminishing in size; it was actually disintegrating and the old woman was not complaining of pain at all anymore.

When Martine left, Anna went over to her baby with a concerned look on her face.

'You have got something to do with this, don't you?' she frowned.

Of course Luke did not answer, but she saw a definite look of satisfaction on the baby's face. A revelation dawned on Anna all of a sudden. It was as if a movie just started with an incredible opening scene.

She remembered the day the big, grey cat came in from outside, bleeding from one ear. While she was looking for some disinfectant, the animal made himself comfortable on the baby's feet in his crib, much to Annals horror.

With a screech she frightened the animal away and he fled out the back door. But a couple of hours later he came back and it was then that she had noticed that there was no blood on his ear anymore. At that stage she forgot about the incident, but it was as if this played a significant part in the discovery of Frau Einfeld's remarkable recovery.

Then there was the incident with one of the local young girls. The child apparently climbed into the attic of a barn. Her foot slipped and she fell off the ladder, breaking her arm.

She too held the baby once.

Shortly after that she complained to her mother that the plaster on her arm was irritating her and that her arm did not hurt anymore. The plaster came off two weeks before it was due and her arm was perfectly healed.

The doctor ascribed this to her age and that she must have looked after herself very well. Anna now knew differently.

It was because of her baby; her baby Luke with his intelligent, dark eyes and understanding look.

A feeling of fear overcame her that made the hair on her neck stand up. This horrible feeling subsided after one glance at the boy, lying so peaceful in his crib.

'*What was going on?*' she wondered.

Then a thought struck her between the eyes as if she were hit by a heavyweight boxer. The boy must have been given to her to fulfil some kind of purpose. It was her duty to look after and take care of him until his mission was fulfilled.

'*Was she being neurotic?*' she thought.

'*No, you're not Anna.*'

Anna knew that she was not and also that the last thought was not her own, but yet another thought projected into her mind. More thoughts like those had entered her mind on previous occasions and now she knew that they came from the little baby boy.

What was she to do?

The fear crept back into her heart as she realised that she did not want to lose the child. Anna picked Luke up as a comfort and that well-known feeling of absolute peace washed all over her.

The boy was given a gentle hug and then put down in his crib again. There was work to be done and Anna knew instinctively that there was not much time left.

She just started typing on the computer when the child cried out in a small voice. Startled by this first ever cry, she jumped up and rushed over to his crib.

'Please,' she said to no-one in particular, 'don't let anything go wrong with my child now!'

The baby stopped crying, though, as soon as he was picked up. He turned his head toward the screen of the computer and Anna's eyes followed his gaze.

Two spaces below the last sentence that she had typed, an image started appearing.

At first it was all scrambled, but it soon developed into a pattern most legible.

It was a date.

03 July.

That was all.

But it was enough for her to know that that was the date. The final chapter of something inevitable was going to happen then.

The image disappeared and she put the child back into his crib and resumed typing. There was not much time until July. The snow has been gone for a week or so already and because of the early Spring, a lot of wild flowers were already sticking out of the fertile ground.

Nobody knew of the turmoil in Anna's mind as the weeks progressed towards the sunny month of July. She decided to keep all of it to herself as she knew that it was something she just could not share with anyone.

Her book came along nicely as she work on it now on a daily basis. *'It just had to be finished by then,'* she kept reminding herself.

In the meantime she took her baby to the hospital as often as she could. Nobody knew her secret and therefore she decided to do as much good as she possibly could. This, of course, left a lot of doctors with a lot of explaining to do. Not only to the patients and their families, but also to colleagues and, most importantly, to themselves.

It was a very strange phenomena and they were looking for answers everywhere.

Anna, on the other hand, occupied most of her time, when she was not writing her book, that is, with Luke. Apart from the regular hospital visits, she tried to spend a lot of quality time with him. Just the two of them in her little, wooden hut in the Alps.

It was the morning of the third of July. Anna had been awake the whole night waiting for another message to appear on her computer. The fact was that she knew there was going to be no message. She started making preparations as if she were going on a picnic. There was a strange, almost telepathic communication between her and Luke by then.

It was due to this that she knew that they would embark on a short, but tiring journey at five o'clock that afternoon.

The day dragged for her as she sat alone in the little hut. She told everybody that she was going to spend some time in Church and that she might spend the night at a friend's house in the city. This white lie made her feel a bit guilty, as it was the second time that she had lied to the villagers. It was not due to the fact that she did not trust anybody, but merely decided that it was for the best.

Anna packed a small back-pack with some sandwiches and water. A quick look at her watch made her heart miss a beat. It was three minutes to five.

They had to go. There was no itinerary; just instincts. Her intuition would lead her and her baby to the venue where this final part of her life would act itself out.

She was not afraid, strangely enough. More curious; oddly relieved that this strange situation in her life was finally coming to an end.

The thought of losing her baby saddened her to the extent that she almost did not open the backdoor to leave everything behind. Anna made sure that the hut was in an impeccable condition and that there were instructions for someone to follow whenever they came to her door.

As soon as they reached the beginning of the seclusion of the trees on the other side of the little stream that flowed at the bottom of the valley, she tied Luke on her back with a blanket, just the way that some black women do in Africa with their little infants.

The back-pack was hanging reversed in front of her chest. Up to then she had only rested once to have a drink of water and to give the child something to drink as well.

As the sun started descending she started feeling quite exhausted. But she had to push on. Something was pushing her. Something that made her forget her sore limbs and to ignore the scratches in her face caused by all the branches of the undergrowth, slapping her from time to time.

After about another forty minutes, Anna decided to take a rest. She untied Luke and put him down on a bed of pine-needles.

Time for a sandwich or two, just to get her strength back, and then she would resume the strenuous journey. She tended to the baby and after another ten minutes of rest, she tied everything up where it belonged.

A sudden rush of energy filled her being. Anna was well-prepared for another couple of hundred miles. That was what she felt, anyway.

After what felt to her like an eternity, she had a quick look at her watch.

It was already dark, but she could still make out the time.

It was twenty minutes to midnight.

Even with her preparations of days in advance, she stupidly forgot to pack the flashlight when they left that morning. That did not seem to be a problem, though. Something or someone was guiding them to their destination.

All of a sudden Anna stopped dead in her tracks.

The journey was quite intense up to then and she had been wondering how far they still had to go.

Then there it was. A clearing in the middle of all those thousands of trees. Not very big; approximately the size of two tennis courts.

Immediately she knew it was the end of the road. Whilst looking around, she untied Luke and the back-pack. She wiped her face with her sleeve to get rid of the beads of sweat running down her forehead. Disappointment came over her, accompanied with a big sigh.

She did not exactly know what she had expected to find. One thing, however, was for sure: she was, at least, expecting someone or something.

The brightness of the night impressed her immensely and with that she looked up at the stars. It was with a shock that she realised that she was on top of the mountain. It had always been one of her dreams to climb up there one day. This part of the mountain was not that high, but she was always intrigued by the beauty of it. Now it was time to sit down and relax, she thought.

A sudden, bright light illuminated the clearing. This was so sudden that Anna almost lost her balance. The first thing she did was to reach out for Luke.
With blood-curdling horror she noticed that he was gone.
'No!' she cried out.
Not exactly realising what was going on and why the flash of lightning, for that was what she thought it was, did not subside, Anna started moving closer to the trees.
Then she heard what she thought was music. Indescribable, sweet tunes came from within the blinding light.
As a tremendous feeling of absolute peace and tranquillity filled her whole being, Anna finally realised why she was there.
All fear had disappeared. She wiped the tears from her eyes and walked into the now diminishing light; only one single beam of brilliant light right in the middle remained.
The realisation of what the situation entailed made her put up her arms in the air in a welcoming gesture.

With that, Anna ascended into the light beam to meet her destiny.

The completed book of Anna was found the following afternoon by a friend of hers. It was neatly stacked on the coffee table with a note on top in her own hand-writing, which explained what was to be done with her manuscript.

There was a brief explanation that she had to leave the valley and that she did not know if she were ever to return. The hut was to be given to the storekeeper with a request that he also took care of her cat.

On the cover page of the manuscript, underneath the title and her name, was a dedication in bold letters:

IN LOVING MEMORY OF ANNA AND HER CHILD